AUTUMN
PUBLISHING

Published in 2024
First published in the UK by Autumn Publishing
An imprint of Igloo Books Ltd
Cottage Farm, NN6 0BJ, UK
Owned by Bonnier Books
Sveavägen 56, Stockholm, Sweden
www.igloobooks.com

0724 002
2 4 6 8 10 9 7 5 3
ISBN 978-1-83771-309-7

Designed by Steve Prosser
Edited by Nicholas Oliver

Printed and manufactured in China

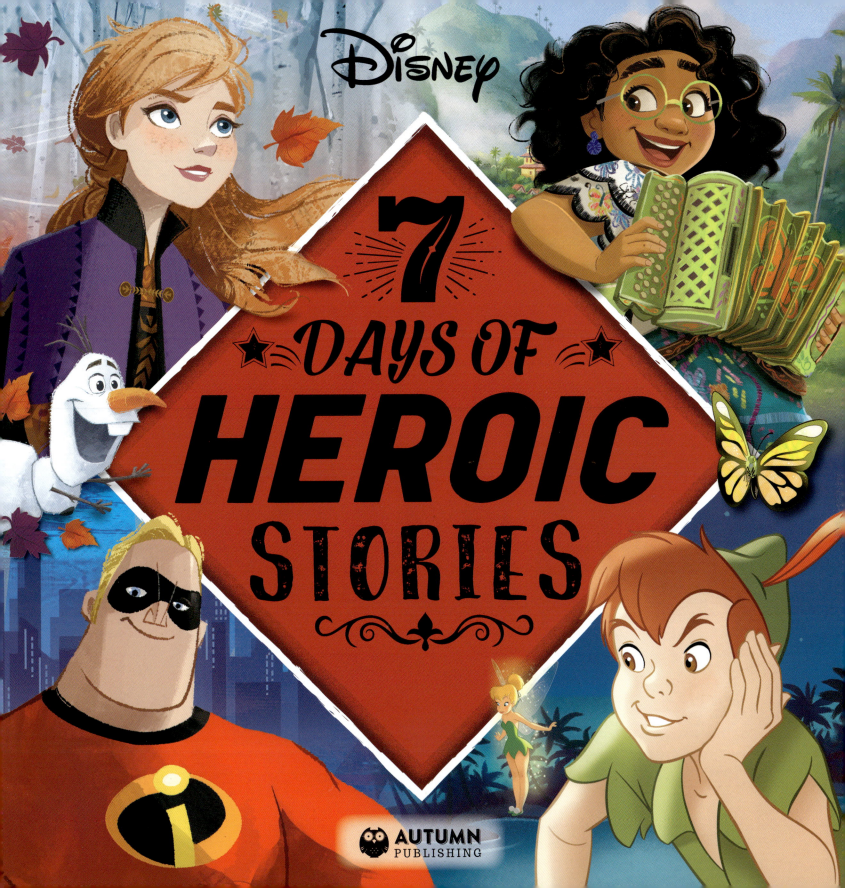

CONTENTS

ENCANTO

MYSTERY OF THE RAINFOREST

The Madrigals were a family like any other. Well, almost. They had magical gifts! And they lived in a wondrous place called an Encanto, which included a village and their magical house, Casita.

Pepa Madrigal had the gift of controlling the weather with her emotions. And today the weather around her was unpredictable! Pepa's daughter, Dolores, who had the gift of hearing everything, had just become engaged. Every time Pepa thought about the wedding reception, her mood switched instantly from happy to worried!

"Mi amor, I know you're nervous about our daughter's big day," said her husband, Felix. "But everything will be perfect. You'll see."

"That's the problem!" cried Pepa. "I wish I could see it, but I can't predict the future…"

That gave Camilo, Pepa and Felix's son, an idea.

"Well, Tio Bruno can," said Camilo, who had the power to shapeshift. He snapped his fingers and changed his youthful face and red curly hair to look just like his uncle's.

Bruno reluctantly agreed to help Pepa peek into the future of her family's anticipated event. Everyone gathered around him, but Bruno's vision didn't show a big party or the design of Dolores's wedding dress.

The vision showed the Encanto looking gloomy and sad… with fallen trees, withered leaves and parched soil. Abuela Alma, the matriarch of the Madrigal family, was worried. She asked Bruno if he knew what was happening. Bruno responded with one last detail: a beautiful Flor de Mayo orchid.

Abuela decided that they should go to the village. Maybe someone there knew what was happening. In town, they met with a few worried families. Señora Osma hadn't been able to prepare her famous empanadas because there wasn't enough corn for the dough. And the Flores family's avocado tree had been without fruit for weeks.

Then, when Mirabel, Abuela's youngest granddaughter, and Antonio, Dolores's little brother, went to buy a green mango with lime and salt at the corner stall, they were told that there were no mangoes or limes.

Camilo and his friend were also disappointed when they couldn't get a refreshing coconut smoothie.

"What do you mean there are no plantains?" Julieta, Mirabel's mama, asked Don Osvaldo Orozco Ortiz at the produce market.

Back at Casita, Julieta continued complaining to Isabela, her eldest daughter and Mirabel's oldest sister, who was desperately trying to replace the withered flowers on all the balconies.

The Madrigals called a family meeting to talk about the mysterious problem. "We must find a solution soon!" said Abuela Alma.

Luisa, Mirabel's other older sister, suggested planting new trees and growing fresh produce, but Isabela told her she had already tried that in town. "The plants, old and new, are barely surviving," she added.

They needed to find the cause!

"I haven't heard the waterfalls in a few days," said Dolores, with her ear pointing towards the mountains.

Antonio watched his family desperately thinking about how to help their beloved Encanto when suddenly his friend Pico, a toucan, clattered in his ear. Antonio knew that the time had come to show them the power of his magical gift.

13

"I know what to do!" Antonio said with excitement. "I need to go to the rainforest."

"Going to the rainforest alone?" asked Abuela. "Papito, I know you're very brave, but that's a big responsibility for a young man like you."

14

Everyone started talking about the baby of the family wanting to solve this huge mystery on his own, until they heard a big roar.

Mirabel broke the awkward silence. "Are we forgetting Antonio's magical gift? He obviously won't do this alone! He has his animal friends," she said.

"Go, Antonio, make your family proud," said Felix, feeling hopeful.

Everyone else agreed.

Pico led the way into the rainforest, while Antonio and the others followed. Along the way, other animals decided to join them.

It wasn't long before they arrived at the edge of a dry river. The waterfall that fed into it was almost dry as well. Only a thin stream of water trickled down the wall of rocks onto the dry dirt.

Mystery of the Rainforest

Antonio noticed a beautiful orchid growing on a tree branch by the waterfall.

A hummingbird buzzed near Antonio and said, "It's a Flor de Mayo, and it's still growing. There must be a reason."

Antonio turned to Pico, the macaw and the hummingbird. "Can you fly up there and look around? Then come and tell me what you see."

At the top of the rocks, the hummingbird got close to the flower, drawn by its scent. The three birds were admiring the orchid's beauty when they finally saw it…

… A large and heavy ceiba tree was blocking the river! The three birds immediately flew back down to tell Antonio.

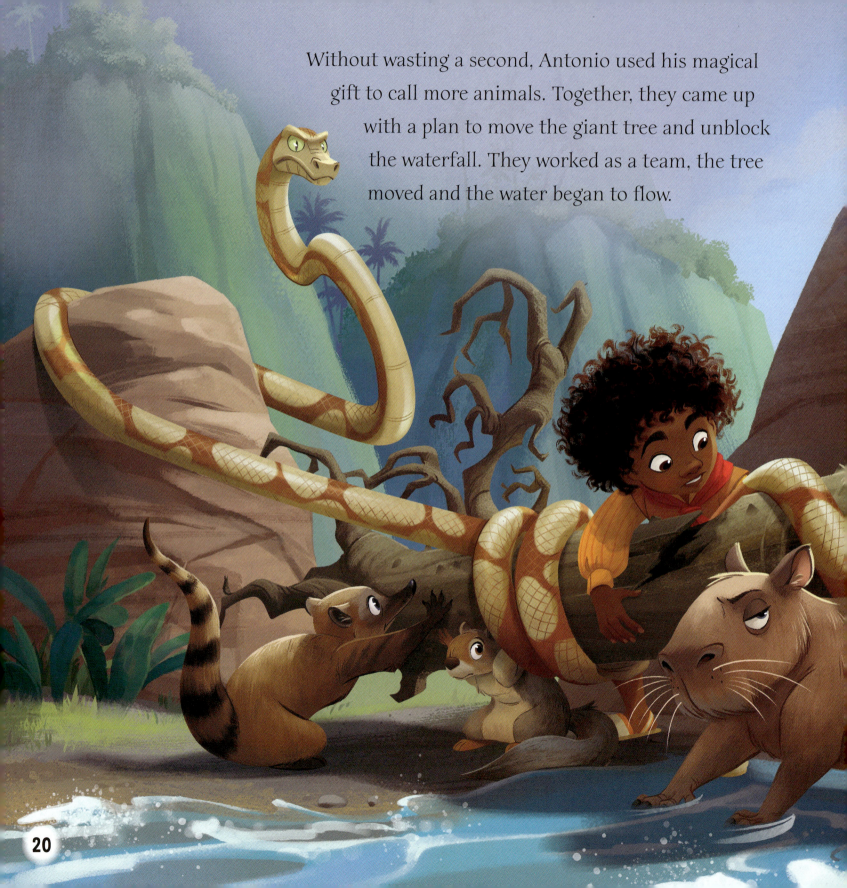

Without wasting a second, Antonio used his magical gift to call more animals. Together, they came up with a plan to move the giant tree and unblock the waterfall. They worked as a team, the tree moved and the water began to flow.

"We did it!" cried Antonio, as he laughed and hugged his animal friends.

He looked gratefully at the orchid, because thanks to it, they were able to discover exactly where the problem was.

Antonio and his animal friends returned to Casita. They shared the good news with the family and the entire community.

"Great job, Antonio!" cried Mirabel. Everyone cheered in celebration.

"Now, let's have a wedding," said Pepa.

"We're so proud of you," said Mirabel. "You helped your community with your magical gift but also with courage and love – the gifts we all have within."

LIGHTYEAR

BUG TROUBLE

It was a special day on T'Kani Prime. Buzz was leading Mo, Izzy and Darby to the Star Command base.

"I can't believe it," said Izzy, excitedly. "It's our first official mission as Space Rangers!"

"I know you're all anxious to show what you can do," said Buzz. "But remember, you still have a lot to learn. You'll need to be alert and ready for anything."

"That won't be a problem," said Mo, confidently. "'Ready for anything' is my middle name!"

Suddenly, a vine wrapped itself around Mo and dragged him away from his friends!

"Now that's what I'm talking about," said Buzz. "Can anyone tell me what you should do in a case like this? Anyone?"

Darby opened her mouth, but Buzz stopped her. "Something that doesn't include a weapon?"

She frowned and shook her head.

Bug Trouble

Buzz walked to the vine and stomped down hard on the slithery arm. The vine released its grip on Mo.

"See? Nice and easy," explained Buzz. "That's how a Space Ranger approaches a mission."

"Thanks, Buzz," said Mo, rising to his feet.

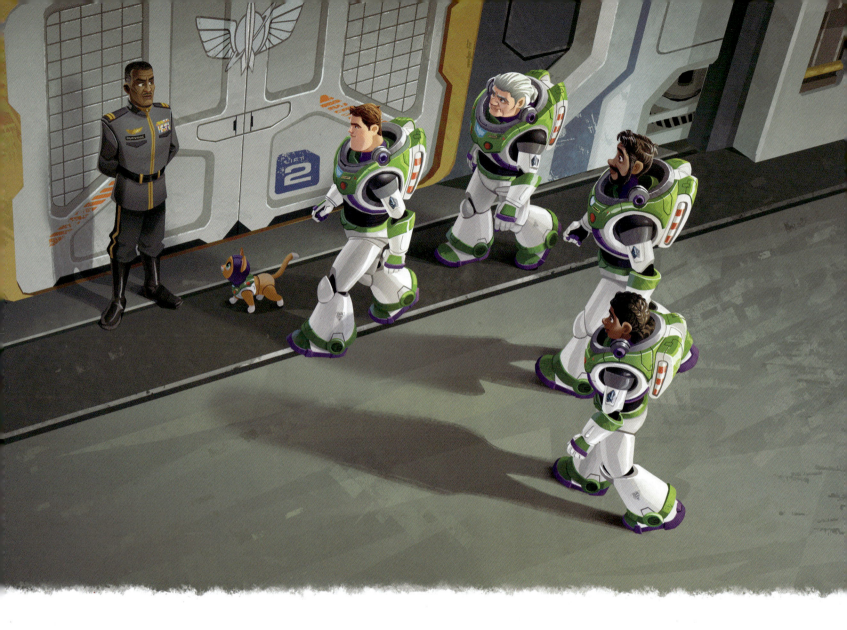

A few minutes later, the Space Rangers reached the large hangar on the edge of the base.

"There you are, right on time," said Commander Burnside. "Captain Lightyear, we have an urgent need for you and your squad."

"We're ready to help," said Buzz.

"More than ready," added Izzy, eagerly. "Beyond ready."

Bug Trouble

"Good," said Commander Burnside. "An unidentified object was detected a short while ago, hurtling towards the planet's Dark Side. Your mission is to investigate this unidentified object and report back."

"Wow! A real mission," Izzy said excitedly, as she settled into one of the pilot seats.

"Let's do everything by the book," said Buzz.

"And be prepared for anything," warned Commander Burnside, as the hatch closed behind Buzz, Izzy, Mo, Darby and Sox.

"Remember," said Buzz, as he started the preflight sequence, "stay close and work together."

The Space Rangers were soon cleared to launch and the ship lifted off.

A short while later, the ship landed flawlessly on the Dark Side of the planet.

"That's funny," said Izzy. "The ship flew a lot smoother than normal."

"Uh, must be the new engines," said Buzz, quickly. He added, "Okay everyone, remain on high alert, and let's go!"

No sooner had the hatch opened, Mo was out of his seat and had bolted outside. He couldn't wait to identify the unidentified object.

"Hey!" Buzz shouted after Mo. "You were supposed to wait until we finished the mission review!"

"Yeah," shouted Darby. "What happened to doing everything by the book?"

"Sorry, Darby," said Mo, shrugging at a shallow trench carved into the soil. At the end of that trench was a glowing purple orb.

"What do you think it is?" asked Mo.

"No idea," replied Darby. "Maybe something that blows up?"

As the two Space Rangers pondered the unidentified object, neither noticed the ominous shapes slowly approaching in the sky behind them.

At the last second, Darby heard a high-pitched buzzing sound.

"Mo, get down!" she shouted, pushing her friend into the dirt.

Suddenly, bugs were upon them!

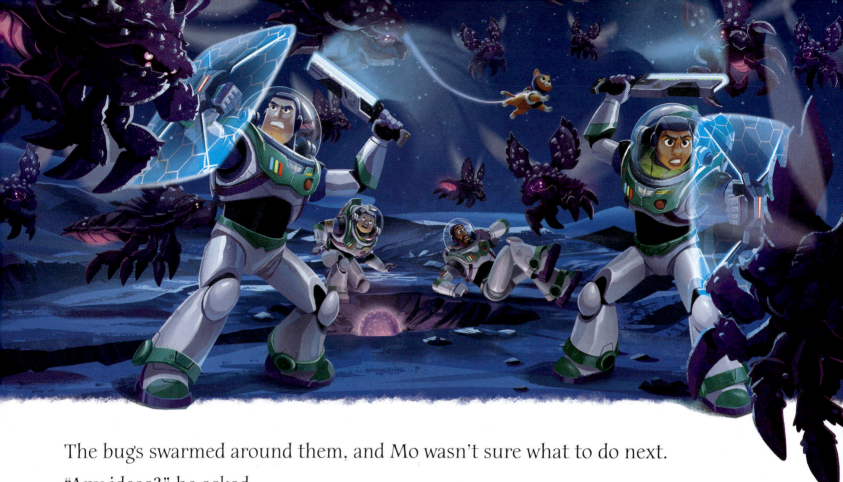

The bugs swarmed around them, and Mo wasn't sure what to do next.

"Any ideas?" he asked.

"Uh, not really," said Darby, checking her suit. "All we have are the standard-issue flares that come with our Space Ranger uniforms. Everything else is still on the ship."

"That's not good," replied Mo.

"Over there, Buzz! I see something."

Mo heard Izzy's voice and looked up. Izzy was running towards them with Buzz by her side. They had shields and laser blades drawn, and they waved them around, driving the bugs away from Mo and Darby.

"Meow, meow, meow. It looks like you require some assistance," said Sox, zipping in on his rocket pack.

Bug Trouble

As the bugs backed off, Buzz approached Mo and Darby with a stern look on his face.

Just as he was about to speak, Izzy jumped in front of him and said, "You can't just run off on your own like that, Mo! You either, Darby! We're a team, and we have to stick together!" Realising she had cut Buzz off, Izzy gave him a sheepish look. "Right, Buzz?"

But Buzz just smiled. "You read my mind, Izzy. That's exactly what I was going to say," he told her.

"Enthusiasm is great," said Buzz. "But Izzy's right. We need to work together as a team."

Sox scanned the purple orb, but the results were inconclusive.

"Curious," said Sox, slowly turning to Buzz. "I am unable to classify this object... or even determine what it's made of. It's almost like it isn't there."

Buzz looked like he was about to say something when a loud buzzing noise came from above.

The bugs had returned, and they had brought friends!

Bug Trouble

As Mo and Darby didn't have any gear, they scrambled behind their teammates for safety. Then, Buzz and Izzy put up their shields and waved their laser blades around to discourage the bugs from attacking.

However, it seemed like the bugs were drawn to the purple orb instead.

"We can't let the bugs take the orb," said Buzz. "We need to bring it back so Star Command can figure out exactly what it is."

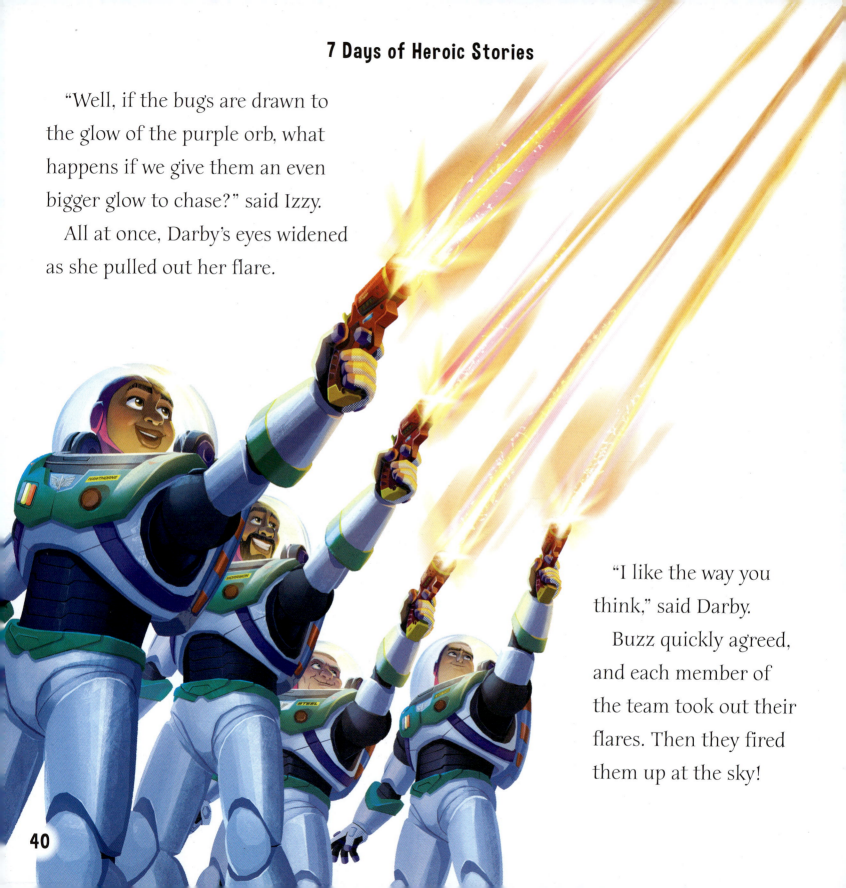

"Well, if the bugs are drawn to the glow of the purple orb, what happens if we give them an even bigger glow to chase?" said Izzy.

All at once, Darby's eyes widened as she pulled out her flare.

"I like the way you think," said Darby.

Buzz quickly agreed, and each member of the team took out their flares. Then they fired them up at the sky!

40

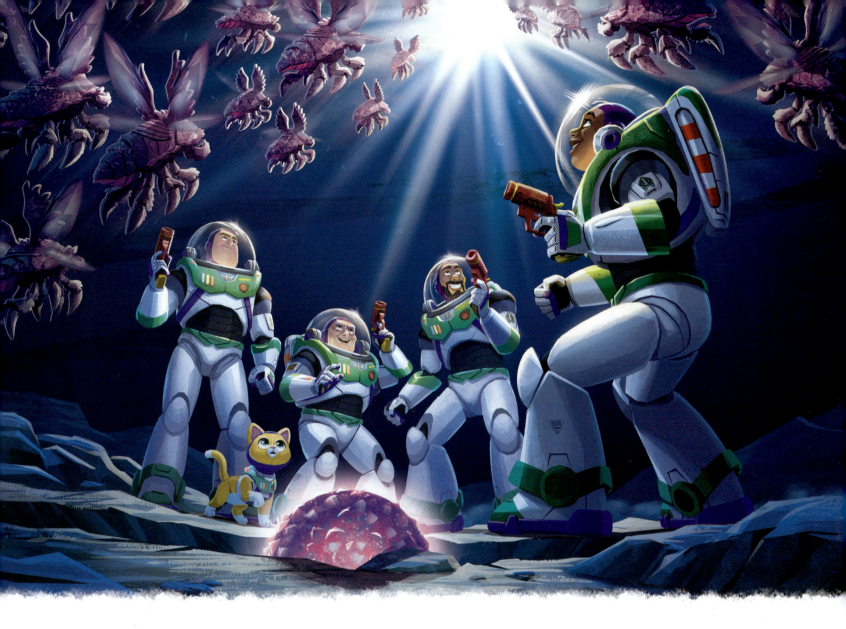

The flares erupted into a giant ball of light, and the bugs lost all interest in the purple orb.

"It's working!" cried Mo.

The bugs soared into the sky, chasing after the fiery glow.

"Great plan!" Buzz said to Izzy before turning to face Mo and Darby. "And great teamwork, too!"

"Now let's get that orb," said Izzy.

But just then, everything went dark. Izzy couldn't see anything except her fellow Space Rangers.

"I knew the Dark Side was dark," observed Mo, "but this is ridiculous."

"What happened?" asked Izzy. "How did it get so dark so fast?"

Then Sox looked at Buzz and said, "I think I might have an idea of what's happening." Buzz grinned as the lights returned.

They weren't on the Dark Side at all. They were still in the hangar, with their ship just behind them. Commander Burnside was standing beside it.

"This hangar is actually a holographic simulator," explained Burnside, "built for Space Ranger training purposes!"

"You knew it wasn't real all along?" Izzy asked Buzz. He nodded.

"The training mission has to feel as real as possible. We may have had a bumpy start, but you showed that we can solve any problem by working together. I'm proud of you," said Buzz.

"It was nothing," said Izzy. "Well, it really was something, wasn't it?"

"It sure was," said Mo.

"Even if we didn't get to blow anything up," agreed Darby.

"You've got yourself quite a team, Buzz," said Commander Burnside. "I think the galaxy's going to be in good hands!"

Disney
Peter Pan

TO THE RESCUE!

One day, Peter Pan and his friends were playing Follow the Leader. As usual, Peter was the leader. Tinker Bell, the Lost Boys, John, Michael and Wendy were following him around Never Land.

Before long, they came to a stream.

"Let's cross it the fun way," suggested Peter.

He grabbed a rope, swung over the water and landed on the other side.

His friends followed, one by one, until only John was left.

"Tallyho!" John cried, and he leapt for the rope. He missed it and fell into the stream. *Splash!*

As Michael helped him out of the water, John grumbled, "Why does Peter always have to be in charge? Just once I'd like to do things my way!"

John decided he wanted to show Peter how brave and clever he was. A little further down the trail, he had an idea. "By Jove," he cried, "I've got it!"

"Got what?" asked Michael.

John said, "You'll see." He took Michael's hand, and together they slipped off into the forest.

To the Rescue!

To the Rescue!

John and Michael disguised themselves as pirates, hopped in a small boat and began to row towards a pirate ship in the harbour. But it wasn't just any ship – it was Captain Hook's! He and Peter Pan were sworn enemies.

"Where are we going?" asked Michael.

"To spy on Captain Hook!" John said excitedly. "We'll take the information back to Peter."

As the boys reached Hook's ship, they heard a noise. *Ticktock!*

"What's that?" asked Michael. Just then, a pair of beady eyes poked up out of the water. It was the Crocodile. Once, he'd swallowed an alarm clock, and now he always made a ticking sound.

"Be careful!" John warned.

John and Michael cautiously climbed over the side of the ship. John spotted two mops and a bucket. He whispered to his brother, "Pretend you're washing the deck."

A moment later, Smee, the first mate, came round the corner. "Ahoy, mateys!" he called. "Can't say that I remember you. But whoever you are, you're doing a fine job!"

To the Rescue!

When Smee was gone, John turned to Michael and said, "Come on, we've got some spying to do. I'm going to look for Hook." He found a telescope and climbed up the rigging.

Smee walked by again. "Do you see anything?" he asked.

"Uh, a storm, actually!" John blurted out.

"I should tell the captain," Smee replied. He hurried off.

John turned to Michael. "This is perfect. He'll lead us right to Captain Hook!"

They followed Smee at a safe distance, hiding behind crates and ropes to avoid being spotted. Finally, they saw him enter a cabin.

"Stand watch. I'll be right back," John whispered to his brother.

When John peered through the porthole of the cabin, he saw Captain Hook. Unfortunately, the pirate saw him, too. Unlike Smee, Hook could tell that John was not a real pirate.

The pirate captain pointed right at John. "I've never seen that one on the crew before! How could you let him onto the ship?"

"Wh-what?" stammered Smee. "B-but, Captain…"

"He's spying on us!" cried Hook. "He could be a friend of that dastardly Peter Pan."

Smee shook his head. "Oh, no, I don't think—"

"Don't just stand there, Smee!" thundered Hook. "Go get him!"

John ducked down from the porthole, grabbed Michael's hand, and said, "I have an idea. Just trust me."

The first mate came scuttling out of the cabin. When he saw the boys, he said, "Oh, it's you! You're not spies, are you?"

"Of course not," said John. "Remember, Mr Smee? You hired us to examine the ship from top to bottom, without alerting the rest of the usual crew. We've been checking the safety of the captain's quarters, and I must say that we're shocked. Why, spies could look through that porthole as easily as I did!"

Smee found them and brought them to see Captain Hook.

"What's the meaning of this?" asked the captain, his hook pointing at John.

"Smee asked us to check the security on board your ship," said John. "He wanted to make sure no one could spy on you."

Hook looked and Smee and smiled. "Is this true?"

Smee couldn't remember asking anyone to check security on board, but seeing that the idea made his captain happy, Smee nodded quickly.

"Good work, Smee," said Captain Hook. "With the attack only three days away, security is more important than ever."

To the Rescue!

"Attack?" said John, trying to hide the concern from his voice.

"Yes," said Hook, "on Peter's hideout." He turned to Smee. "Release them, Smee. We've got work to do."

As soon as they were outside, John whispered to Michael, "We have to warn Peter!" Quickly, they climbed over the side of the ship and began rowing towards shore.

To the Rescue!

Captain Hook laughed as he watched the two boys through his telescope.

"They'll lead us straight to Pan!" he said.

Smee straightened his glasses. "Y-you mean, they really were spies?"

"Of course," the pirate replied. "They're some of Pan's little friends. They don't know it yet, but now they are working for us!"

A short time later, John and Michael reached the shore.

"My plan worked!" John cried. "Wait till Peter hears!"

Ticktock. Ticktock. "Uh-oh," Michael said." "I hear ticking. Like a clock. Like a clock in a crocodile. Like a clock in a crocodile that follows Captain Hook!"

John looked back out at the sea, and once again, he saw a pair of beady eyes and a hint of green scales poking out of the water.

"It is the Crocodile," he said with a gasp. "And that can only mean..."

The boys looked at each other. "Hook!" they said. "Run!"

They scrambled up a hill towards Peter's hideout, with John leading the way.

When John reached the top, he called, "This way, Michael!"

But there was no answer...

"Michael?" John said, glancing over his shoulder.

Captain Hook stood at the bottom of the hill. Beside him, two pirates had Michael in their clutches. "Don't hurt my brother!" shouted John.

"Go tell Peter and Wendy!" cried Michael. "Don't stop!"

Swallowing his fear, John ran as fast as he could to get Peter Pan.

A few minutes later, John burst into Peter's hideout. "Come quick!" he yelled. Peter, Wendy and the others gathered round him.

John told them what had happened to Michael and that Hook was planning to attack. "I'm sorry," said John. "I thought Hook and Smee believed our story. I didn't mean to put Michael in harm's way."

Peter shook his head. "If Hook knew where I lived, why would he have followed you? I think it was a trick."

"He knew Michael and I weren't pirates?" asked John.

To the Rescue!

"I'm afraid so," Peter said.

John groaned. "I've made a terrible mess of things. Will you help?"

"Sure. I've got a plan," Peter replied. "Let's go!"

On the pirate ship, Smee tied Michael to a chair, while Hook tried to find out where the secret entrance to Peter's hideout was.

Just then, they heard a girl say, "Captain Hook?" It was Wendy. She was standing on the ship's plank.

"Watch the boy, Smee," Hook said. "I'll be right back!"

As soon as Hook was gone, John looked into the porthole.

"Not you again!" Smee exclaimed as he chased after John.

With Hook and Smee distracted, the Lost Boys hurried inside and untied Michael. Then they carried him to the side of the ship and climbed down into a boat that was waiting below.

John led Smee on a wild chase around the ship's deck, bobbing and weaving round crates and barrels until the pirate was huffing, puffing and struggling to keep up. When he saw the boys were all safe, John opened his umbrella, leapt over the side of the ship and floated down to join them. "I'm sorry, Michael," John told his brother. "I shouldn't have put you in danger like that. Will you forgive me?"

"Of course!" said Michael. "After all, you did come to my rescue. But where are Peter and Wendy?"

"Don't worry," John told him. "They're just helping out with the rescue plan."

Then the Lost Boys cast off and headed for shore.

Meanwhile, on the ship's plank, Captain Hook reached out to grab Wendy. Suddenly, a green blur streaked through the air and scooped her up. It was Peter Pan!

"Blast you, Pan!" Hook cried. He lunged forwards and fell overboard, snagging the plank with his hook. "Smee!" Hook cried as the Crocodile circled below.

Later that evening, Peter and his friends sat in their hideout, talking about the rescue.

"When Michael and I met Captain Hook, how did he know we weren't pirates?" asked John.

"Pirates don't usually carry umbrellas," Peter said, smiling.

Everyone laughed. What an adventure they'd had!

"Next time, I won't attempt a mission without telling all of you first!" said John. "After all, we work best when we're together."

TRAINING TUK TUK

Every afternoon, Raya and her father, Benja, met for tea.

Lately, Raya had been spending most of her days training, and she often lost track of time. "Sorry I'm late, Ba," said Raya, rushing in. "But I'm so close." She picked up a dessert and took a bite. "I'll be a Guardian of the Dragon Gem soon."

She had been working for months to prove she had the skills needed to protect the Gem of the last dragon, and it was almost her chance to show it.

"I'm proud of your hard work," said Benja. "But you must remember to make time for other things. Balance is important."

"There is more to being a good warrior than training," added Benja.

Raya nodded. "Yes, Ba."

"I have a surprise for you," he said, handing her a basket.

Raya peered inside to see a small armoured ball.

She picked it up and held it in her hand. Two furry legs appeared, and a big pair of eyes looked up at her. Raya gasped.

"His name is Tuk Tuk," said Benja. "And it will be up to you to take care of him."

Raya set Tuk Tuk down and watched as he took a few clumsy steps. A beetle landed in his path and charged towards him. Alarmed, Tuk Tuk tried to get out of the strange creature's way. Instead he accidentally flipped over and landed on his shell, where he struggled to get up.

"I gotcha," said Raya, turning him over.

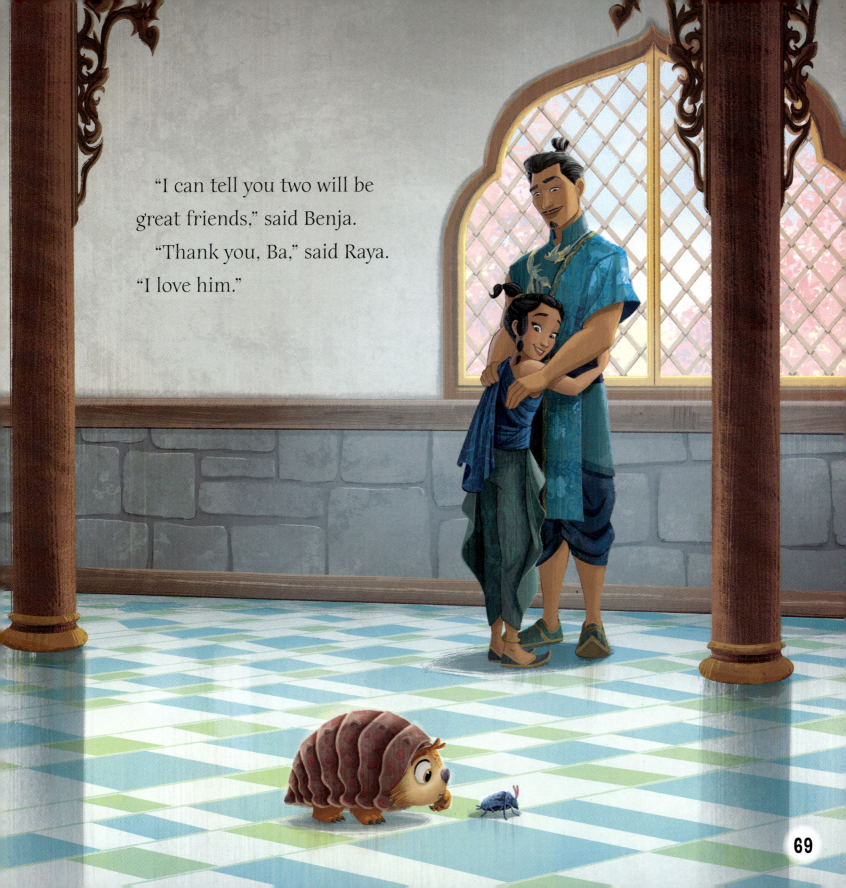

"I can tell you two will be great friends," said Benja.

"Thank you, Ba," said Raya. "I love him."

Raya tried to get Tuk Tuk to follow her as she headed off to train.

She led him to her favourite obstacle course… one of her favourite training spots. But at the obstacle course, Tuk Tuk seemed to take interest in everything but the course.

Raya spent nearly all her time taking care of him.

So Raya built a mini obstacle course just for Tuk Tuk. His first challenge was to climb the netting, but he ended up chasing a butterfly.

Then he was supposed to balance on the logs, but he ended up stuck on his back again.

Finally, Tuk Tuk was just supposed to cross the board, but he fell asleep!

Training Tuk Tuk

The next day, as they prepared to have tea, Raya told her father about what had happened at the mini obstacle course. "I don't know what to do, Ba…" she said with a sigh.

"Be patient," said Benja. "You are still getting to know each other. Everyone is good at something. Once you figure out what Tuk Tuk is good at, you'll know what to do."

Raya shrugged. "I want to train Tuk Tuk, but he only seems good at getting distracted."

"Patience," said Benja. He gestured towards the table. "Now let's have our dessert."

But their bowls were empty!

74

Training Tuk Tuk

"Tuk Tuk ate our food!" cried Benja.

"How did he…" began Raya, looking at Tuk Tuk, who innocently gazed back at her. "You are sneaky," she added.

"And clever," added Benja.

A grin appeared on Raya's face. "I know what to do. I need more food!" She raced into the kitchen.

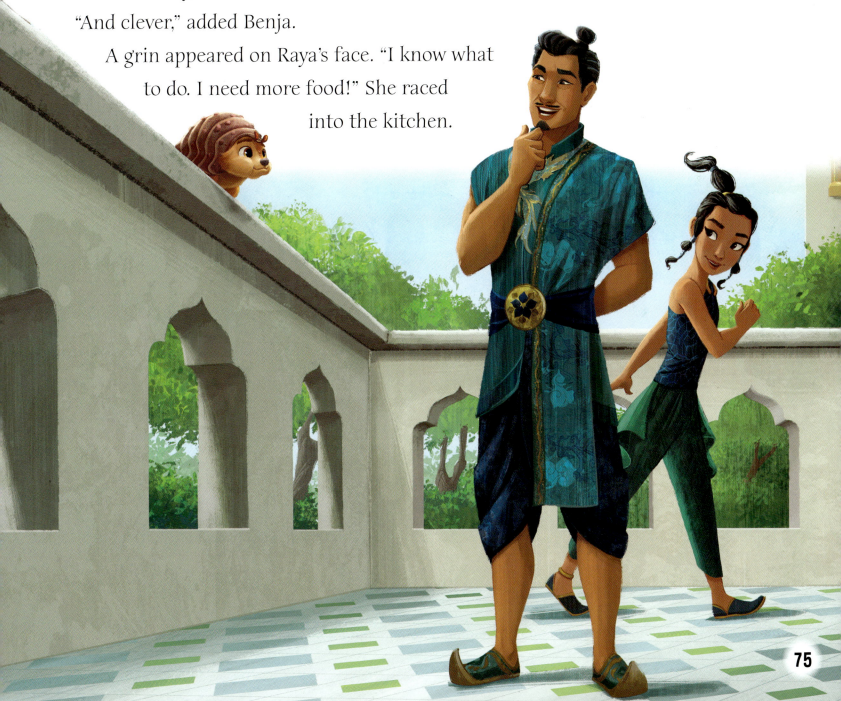

When Raya returned, she called Tuk Tuk, but he didn't budge. Then she held up a coconut treat and tried again.

In a flash, he rolled off the ledge, landing at Raya's feet!

Training Tuk Tuk

She broke off a piece of the treat and gave it to him. Then she told him to follow her.

"Bye, Ba!" said Raya, starting off. "Let's go train, Tuk Tuk. Come on!"

Benja watched as Tuk Tuk raced after her.

Using bits of food, Raya got Tuk Tuk to move through the course. Every time he made it past an obstacle, she gave him a treat.

Training Tuk Tuk

Soon he was getting through the whole thing without stopping once.

He quickly became better and better.

One day, after Tuk Tuk had zoomed past every obstacle, Raya said, "It's time."

Raya brought him to her course, and as she practised, he followed. The two worked together every day, having fun, improving their skills...

Training Tuk Tuk

… and eating plenty of coconut treats!

One night, Raya looked at Tuk Tuk and said, "Let's do this."

She put on her gloves and mask, and tied her hair back. With her best friend by her side, she crept into the night. Raya was ready to show she had the strength and intelligence to pass all the obstacles, reach the inner platform where the last dragon's Gem was kept and prove herself a Guardian of the Dragon Gem.

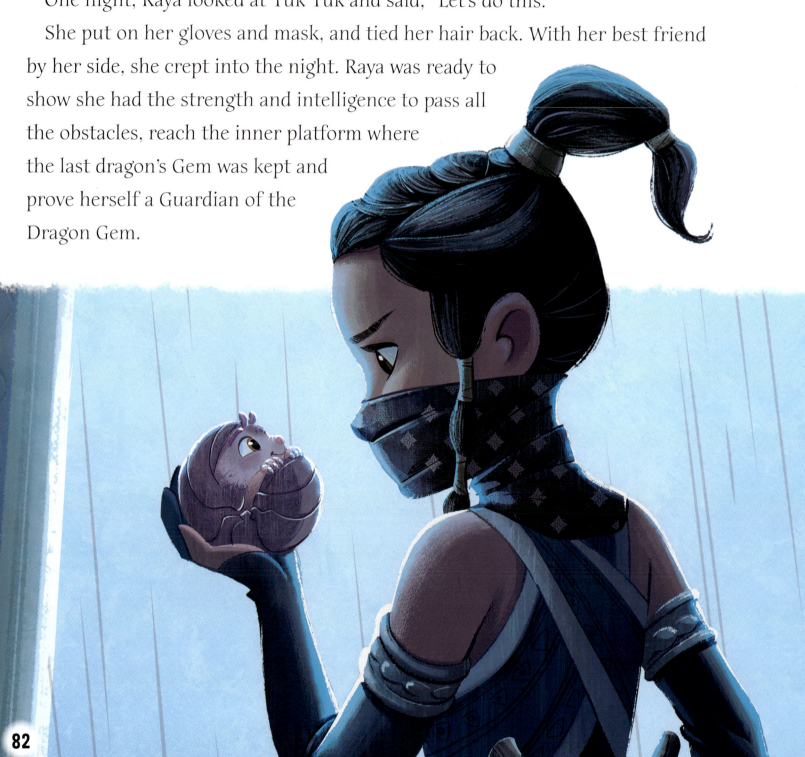

FROM THE MOVIE

Disney · PIXAR
ONWARD

MIGHTY MUM

Early one morning, Ian, Barley and Laurel Lightfoot arrived at Manticore's Tavern. The Manticore directed the construction crews as they tore away the tavern's modern façade. Soon it would be returned to its former glory as a quest landmark.

"Thank goodness you're here!" exclaimed the Manticore. "The reopening is coming up fast, and I need all the help I can get."

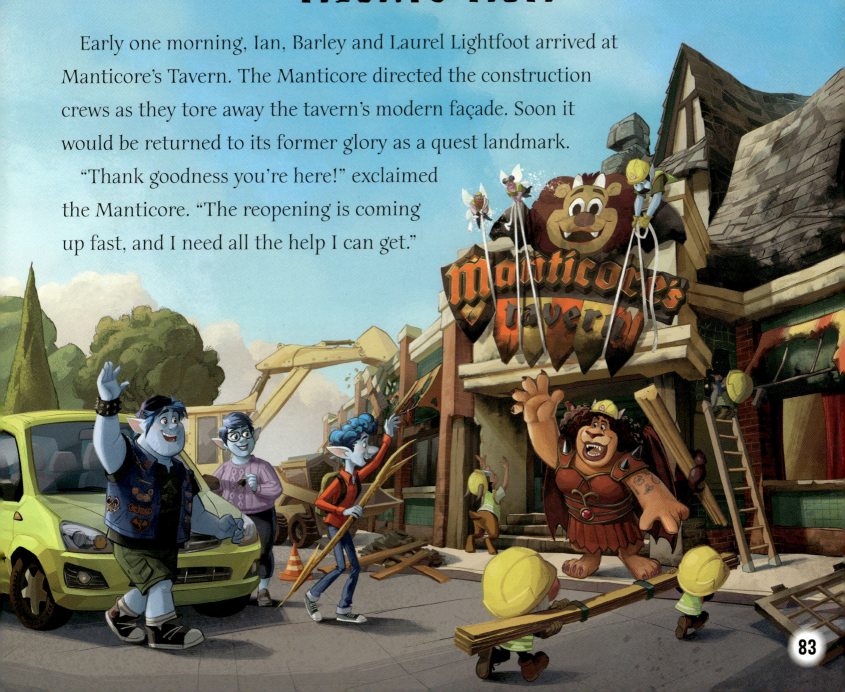

The Lightfoots didn't waste any time. Ian used magic to summon equipment from the supply closet. Laurel grabbed a sledgehammer and began to tear down a wall. A few spiders crawled out of the hole she had made.

"Ugh!" Laurel cried. "I hate spiders."

Ian laughed. "Mum, you fought a dragon. Spiders are nothing!"

As Laurel got back to work, she came across an old nameplate.

"'Chantar's Talon'," she read. "Where does this go?"

"Nowhere. I never actually found the talon!" The Manticore laughed. "I had always planned to go on a quest to retrieve it, but I got too busy running the tavern."

"According to legend," Ian said, pulling the Quests of Yore book from his backpack, "Chantar's Talon brought endless prosperity."

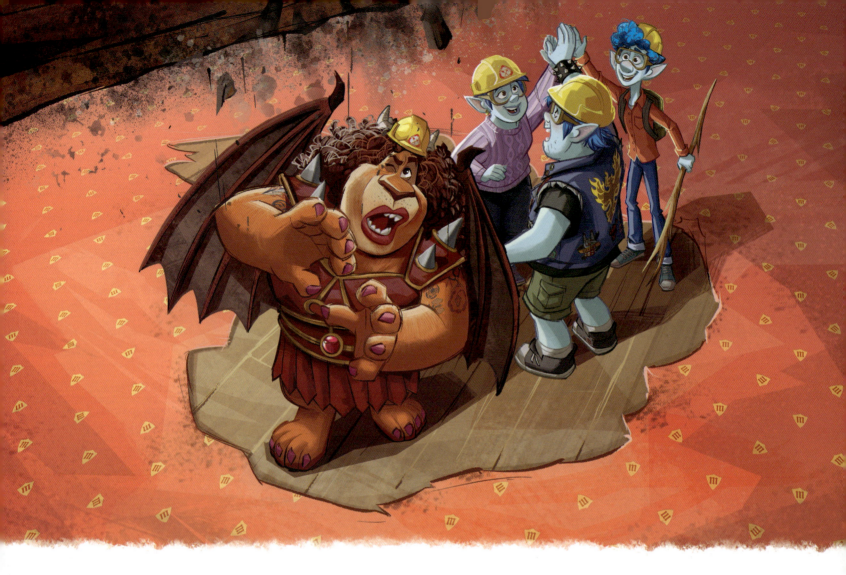

Just then, the debris rained down from the ceiling.

The Manticore sighed. "I could use some of that prosperity right now. But there's no time to go on a quest! This place will fall to pieces without me."

"We'll find it and display it at the grand reopening!" Laurel said.

"A family quest!" cheered Barley.

"I love that idea!" exclaimed the Manticore. "The map burned up in the fire, but the Whispering Elms will know the way."

As the group prepared to leave, Laurel realised something. "How dangerous will this be?"

"Oh, it'll be easy for you three," said the Manticore. "But never forget: you have to take risks in life to have an adventure!"

"Fear not!" exclaimed Barley. "The Lightfoot fellowship shall conquer any challenge with sheer wit and strength!"

"We will bestow the glorious Chantar's Talon upon thee!" added Ian.

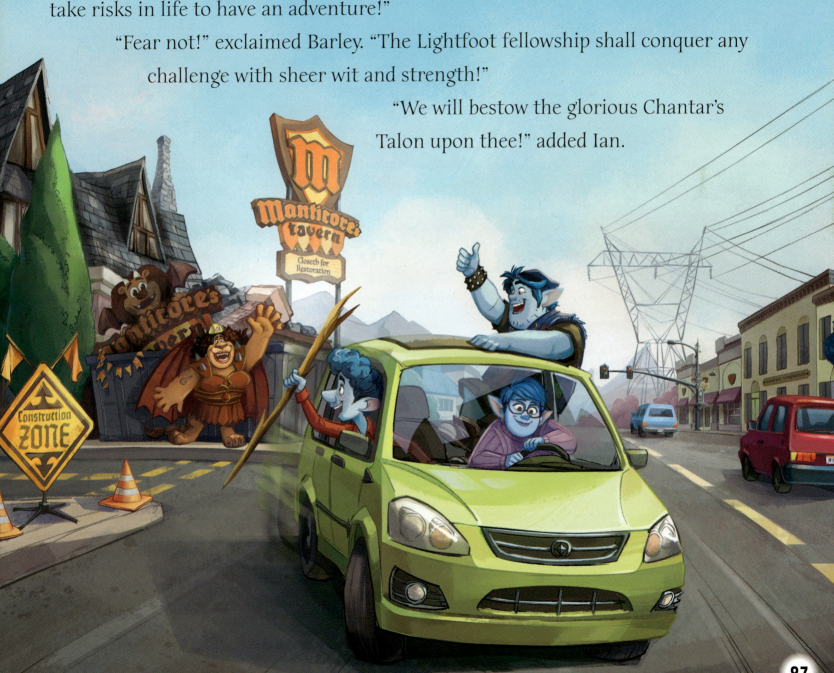

7 Days of Heroic Stories

When Laurel, Ian and Barley arrived at the supermarket, they found the Whispering Elm and asked it if it knew where to find Chantar's Talon.

"Wow," said the Elm. "That really takes me back. "You must reach the centre of the labyrinth and face the mighty Minotaur!"

The Elm explained the labyrinth was now a shopping centre, so they might have trouble finding the entrance after so many years.

Mighty Mum

The Lightfoots headed to the shopping centre, eager to find out more.

Once inside, Laurel found a member of staff. "Excuse me? Could you tell us how to get to the middle of the shopping centre?"

Barley stared. "Aren't you the guardian of the labyrinth?"

"I'm not in that business any more, kid," the Minotaur said dully. "Make a right then a left and another right."

7 Days of Heroic Stories

The Lightfoots followed the guard's instructions. But all they found was a children's play area. Kids screamed and ran every which way.

Laurel pointed to the giant ball pit. "There's a Minotaur in the centre! That can't be a coincidence."

Mighty Mum

The family jumped into the pit and manoeuvred through the chaos. A golden crest on the Minotaur's pedestal caught Ian's eye. Laurel pulled the padding away from the pedestal and found a blocked archway.

"The Animate Spell should do the trick," said Ian. "*Presto Avar!*"

The bricks began moving away, leaving an opening in the archway.

After the Lightfoots entered, the bricks slammed back into place. They were plunged into total darkness.

"*Flame Infernar!*" shouted Ian. A bright flame ignited at the top of the staff, illuminating an ancient stone staircase.

Barley created a torch and led the way. "Looks like the only way out is forward."

The group made their way to a massive chamber.

"Something doesn't feel right to me," said Laurel, coming to a halt. "Why haven't we run into anyone… or anything?"

She found a discarded suit of armour on the ground and put it on. "Maybe this will come in handy!"

"I'll see if the Danger Detection Spell can help us," said Ian.

The top of the staff glowed a deep, ominous red.

Suddenly, a giant spider scooped up all three of them and weaved them tighter and tighter into its web. Ian's staff clattered to the floor, out of reach.

"The Manticore said this quest would be easy!" cried Ian.

"Why did it have to be a spider?" added Laurel.

Just when all hope seemed to be lost, Barley spotted something in an alcove below them.

"Chantor's Talon!" he cried. "It's right there!"

Mighty Mum

Laurel used a sharp edge of the armour to cut them down. Although she managed to escape, the boys were still trapped in the web! She dashed towards an axe propped up against a wall at the far side of the chamber and snatched it up.

Laurel faced the creature. "If I can defeat a dragon, I can defeat you!" She dodged, weaved and rolled so quickly that the spider became disorientated.

With the spider confused, Laurel freed
the boys from the web.

"Way to go, Mum!" cheered Barley.

Ian grabbed his staff. They needed
a diversion to escape.

96

"*Cumulo Mystara*!" cried Ian.

The room filled with a thick fog. As the spider struggled to see, Laurel sprinted to the alcove and grabbed the talon.

"Got it!" she shouted. "Now let's get out of here!"

The Lightfoots ran out of the chamber just as the last of the fog cleared.

The family managed to find
their way out of the tunnel and
the shopping centre. Exhausted
and exhilarated, they arrived
back at the tavern.

The Manticore was thrilled
to see that they had completed
the quest.

"You did it!" she exclaimed.
"Like I said, piece of cake, right?"

Laurel, Barley and Ian looked
at each other and smiled.
The Manticore placed the talon
on the wall along with her
other relics.

"I'm finally ready for my grand
reopening!" she said. She looked
around at the construction
chaos. "Well… almost."

"I gotta hand it to you, Mum," said Barley. "That was pretty cool."

"We're lucky to have such a fearless and mighty mum," added Ian.

Laurel smiled and gave them a big hug.

"Let's plan our next adventure! Nothing will stand in the way of the Lightfoots. Not even a—"

"Spider!" cried Ian and Barley together.

A DAY OUT WITH MUM

Helen knew Bob was still a little worn out from taking care of everything in her absence. "Why don't you go do something fun?" she suggested. "Take a little time for yourself and—"

Bob sprang up, kissed her on the cheek and headed towards the door. "Thanks, honey!" he shouted. "See you guys later!"

After breakfast, Helen had an idea. "Hey, Vi—"

"Yes, I'll watch Jack-Jack while you take Dash to track practice," said Violet.

"Actually, I was going to ask if you wanted to come with me," said Helen. "After we drop Dash off, I'll take you shopping for something nice to wear on your first date with Tony."

"I don't know," said Violet. "I was just going to wear something like… this." She gestured to her outfit.

"Come on," said Helen. "It'll be some mother-daughter fun. You know, we can bond."

"Okay, Mum," Violet said with a chuckle.

Helen and the kids piled into the car and headed out.

They soon arrived at Dash's school and wondered why they were the only ones in the car park. "Oh, no," said Dash. "I forgot practice is cancelled today!"

"Well… you can help with Jack-Jack," said Helen, upbeat. "Then Vi and I can focus on shopping."

"Great… babysitting," said Dash under his breath.

"Badadbaada," Jack-Jack babbled happily.

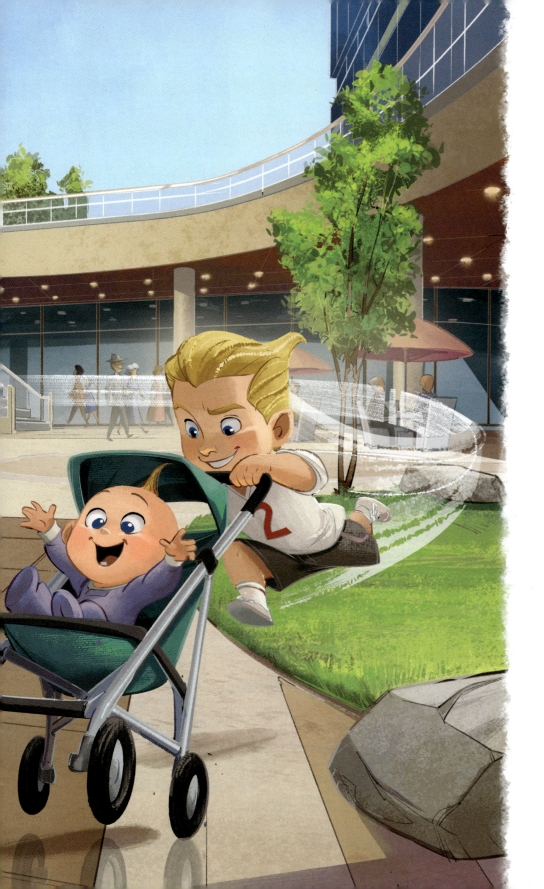

Dash dragged his feet as he pushed Jack-Jack in the pram.

Whenever Helen and Violet stopped to look in a shop window, he zoomed around the shopping centre. He got away with it for a little while before his mother noticed.

"Dash!" she yelled. "No running with the baby! You'll get him all worked up."

Dash knew he wasn't supposed to use his powers in public for fun. "I'm battling the evils of boredom," he explained.

Helen raised her eyebrows and said, "Stop."

Helen and Violet began picking out things for Violet to try on, but Dash and Jack-Jack kept distracting them. When Jack-Jack spotted the shopping centre's carousel, he whined and shouted, "Babababa!"

Dash kept groaning as if he were in pain, until Helen handed him some money.

"Take your brother on the carousel and go enjoy yourselves," she said, forcing a smile. "Meet us at the fountain in an hour."

"Thanks!" said Dash, who then wheeled a laughing and clapping Jack-Jack away.

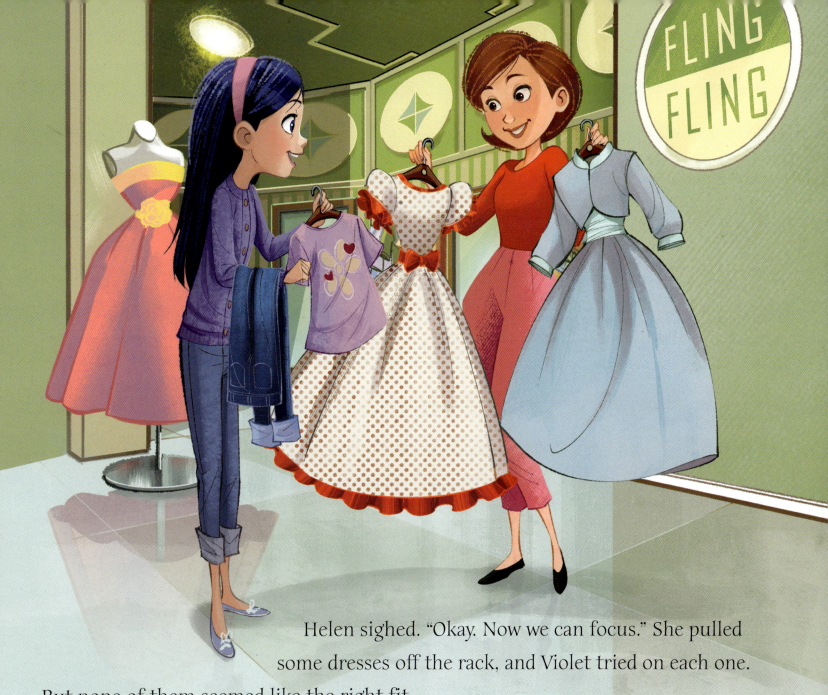

Helen sighed. "Okay. Now we can focus." She pulled some dresses off the rack, and Violet tried on each one. But none of them seemed like the right fit.

They went into another shop, and Violet found an outfit she liked. "This is cute," she said.

"But so casual," said Helen. She held up a couple of dresses. "Look at these!"

Violet smiled and took them into the changing room.

Meanwhile, Dash and Jack-Jack were having a blast. First, they rode on the carousel.

Then, Dash bought his brother the biggest lollipop he could find. Unable to decide what he wanted, Dash bought all sorts of sweets for himself.

At the fountain, Helen felt sad that they hadn't found Violet anything for her to wear on her date.

Soon after, Dash showed up with Jack-Jack. "Sorry we're late!" he cried.

Before Helen could reply, an alarm blared from the jewellery shop.

The family slapped on their
masks and revealed their Supersuits.
The Incredibles were ready for action!
At the jewellery shop, the owner explained how the thief took
the jewellery and money from the till, before literally vanishing.
Elastigirl and the kids looked for clues.
"Do you think the villain can turn invisible like Vi?" asked Dash.
Suddenly, another shop's alarm blared! The Supers took off towards it.

BWOOP! BWOOP! BWOOP! A chorus of alarms rang from every corner of the shopping centre!

"Maybe it's a whole team of thieves," said Elastigirl.

"Or maybe he can multiply, like Jack-Jack," said Violet.

Hearing that, Jack-Jack multiplied, and each baby wandered off in a different direction.

A moment later, they heard Jack-Jack babbling angrily, and Elastigirl yelled, "Food court!"

Elastigirl and Violet collected as many Jack-Jacks as they could while Dash raced to find the thief.

Dash spotted the burglar and could tell right away: he was definitely a super villain. As Dash rushed towards him, he vanished in a flash of light! Dash didn't notice as the burglar reappeared right behind him.

Elastigirl entered, carrying an armful of Jack-Jacks, and tried to stretch-grab the villain, but he disappeared and reappeared at a till behind her!

"Elastigirl?" the thief said, chuckling. "I had to pick the shopping centre where Elastigirl shops?" She turned and reached for him, but he vanished. "Name's Blindspot," he said, reappearing at another till. Dash raced towards him as he disappeared again.

115

Then Violet saw Blindspot.

"Coffee shop!" she yelled, pointing at him.

Dash and Elastigirl ran over. All the Jack-Jacks in Elastigirl's arms merged back into one and headed towards Violet.

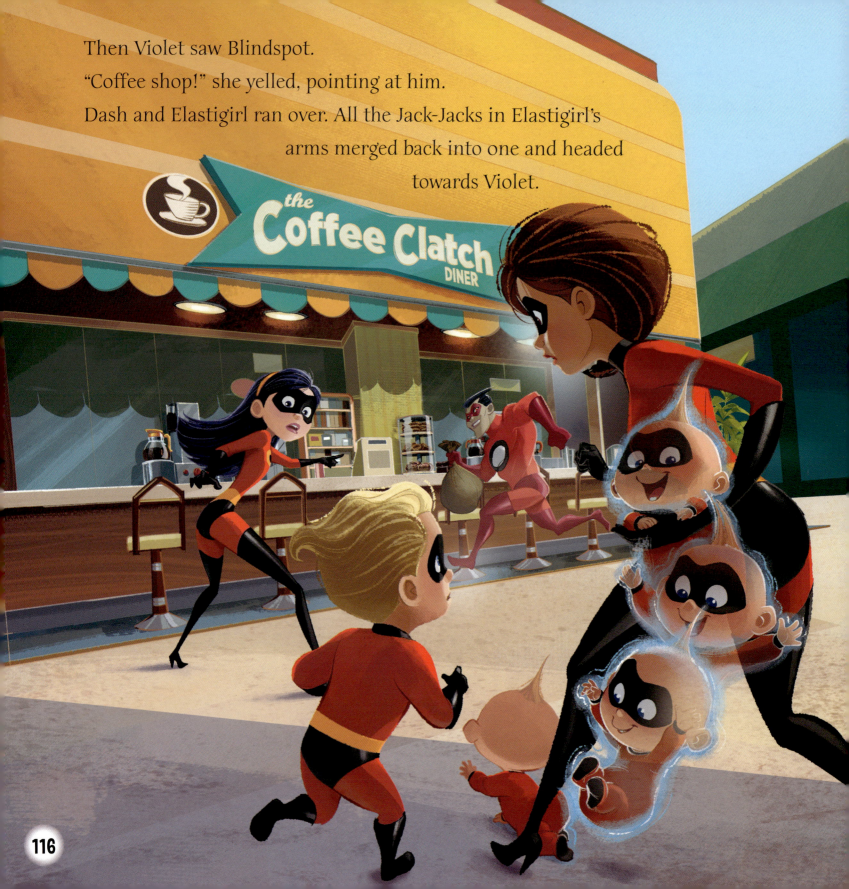

Violet scooped up Jack-Jack, who used his laser eyes against Blindspot. But the villain disappeared again!

Even with his super speed, Dash wasn't fast enough to catch the vanishing villain.

Elastigirl stretched and wound her body through the shopping centre, creating a labyrinth of traps, hoping to trip him up. But Blindspot managed to disappear and reappear his way through them with ease.

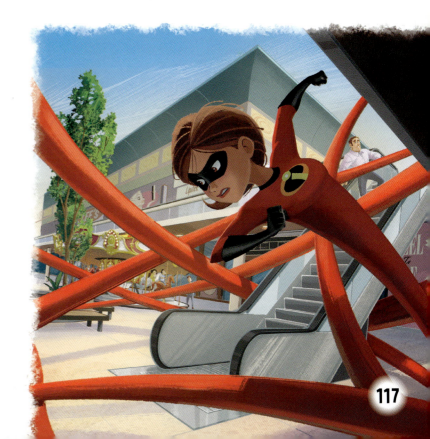

Then, Violet caught Blindspot's reflection in one of the carousel mirrors. His eyes opened wide, and he began to run. Dash approached and Blindspot disappeared again. Violet had an idea.

She found Blindspot stealing cash from a clothes shop till and kicked all the changing room doors open, revealing ther mirrors inside. Once again, Blindspot looked up at a mirror, caught.

Suddenly, Dash and Elastigirl realised what Violet already knew... he was travelling through their blind spots!

A Day Out With Mum

The family used mirrors so it was impossible for Blindspot to disappear.
Violet then threw a force field over the villain, trapping him inside.

It was then Elastigirl noticed a dress in the window, and pointed it out to Violet.

"I'm sorry to disappoint you, Mum," said Violet. "But I don't really like dresses."

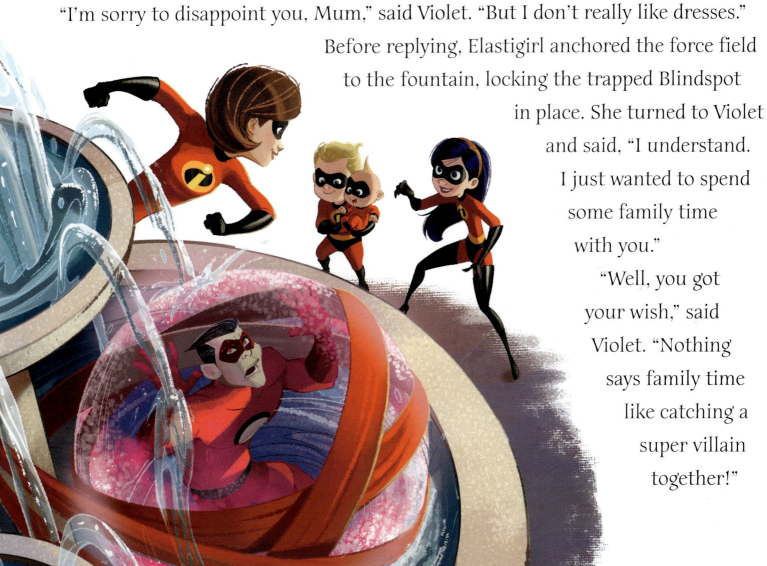

Before replying, Elastigirl anchored the force field to the fountain, locking the trapped Blindspot in place. She turned to Violet and said, "I understand. I just wanted to spend some family time with you."

"Well, you got your wish," said Violet. "Nothing says family time like catching a super villain together!"

With Blindspot safe in custody, the family changed and headed home.

"You know what I wore on my first date with your father?" Helen asked Violet.

Violet shook her head. "What?"

"I have no idea," said Helen. "Clothes don't really matter. So wear something you like. You'll look fantastic no matter what."

Disney FROZEN II

WELCOME HOME

Lieutenant Destin Mattias had been one of Arendelle's most honourable officers. When King Runeard of Arendelle led a group of Arendellians to the celebration of the dam they had built for their neighbours, the Northuldra, Mattias was by his side.

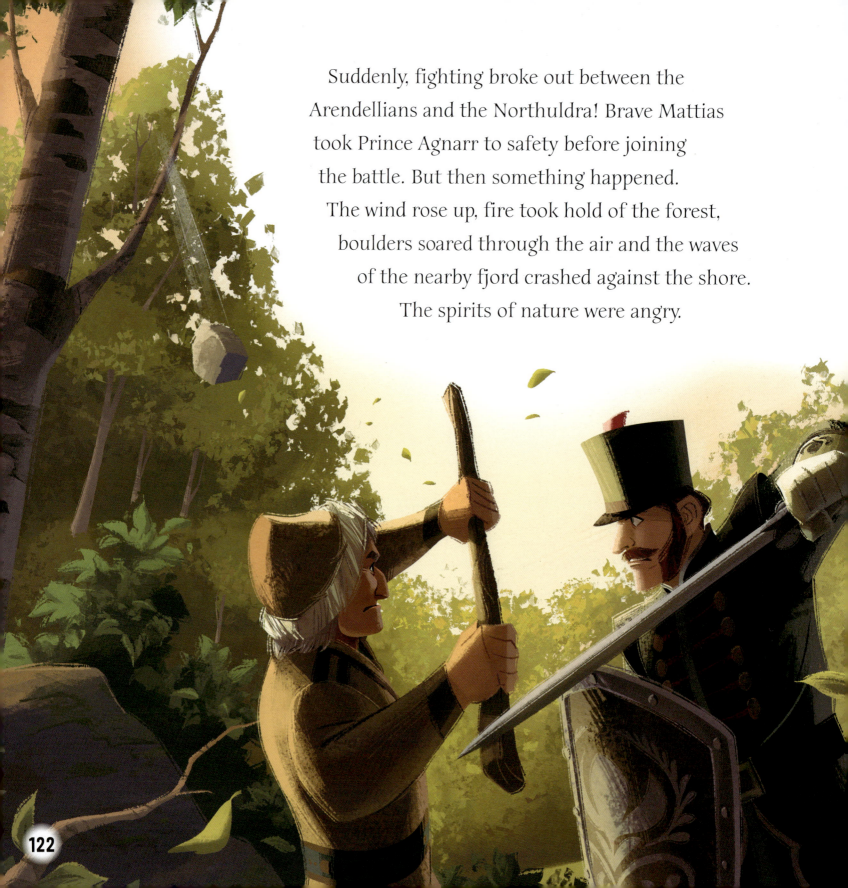

Suddenly, fighting broke out between the
Arendellians and the Northuldra! Brave Mattias
took Prince Agnarr to safety before joining
the battle. But then something happened.
The wind rose up, fire took hold of the forest,
boulders soared through the air and the waves
of the nearby fjord crashed against the shore.
The spirits of nature were angry.

The spirits created a mysterious mist that shrouded the entire forest for over thirty years, allowing no one to enter and no one to leave, until Anna and Elsa restored harmony between the Northuldra and the Arendellians.

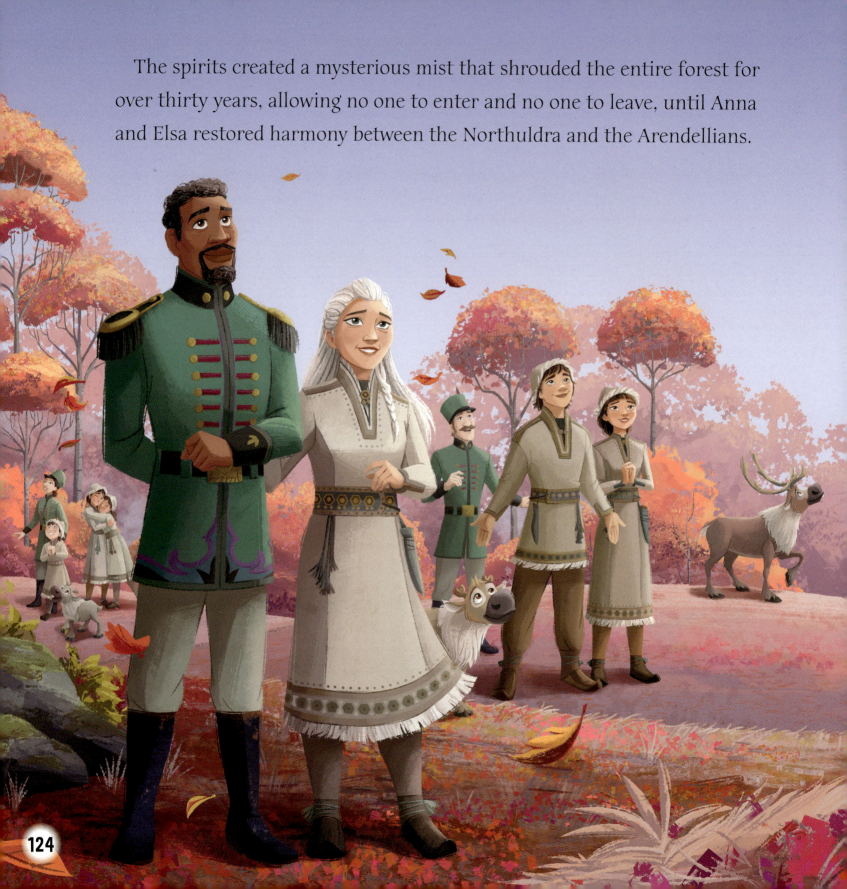

Welcome Home

Now, at long last, Mattias was coming home to Arendelle... and to those he'd left behind, like Halima. When Mattias first met her, she'd worked at Hudson's Hearth. Now, she owned it.

7 Days of Heroic Stories

"A lot has changed," Mattias said to Anna. Anna nodded towards Halima. "And fortunately, some things haven't."

126

Welcome Home

Though he'd grown up in Arendelle, it would take time for Mattias to familiarise himself with all the changes in the kingdom since he'd been gone. And now that Anna was queen, Arendelle looked a little different to her as well.

7 Days of Heroic Stories

Anna had an idea that just might help them both.

"How about a hero's welcome, with a guided tour of the new Arendelle?" she asked.

"A hero's welcome is not necessary, Your Majesty, but I would certainly love the tour," Mattias said, bowing low. "And perhaps we could take photographs along the way?"

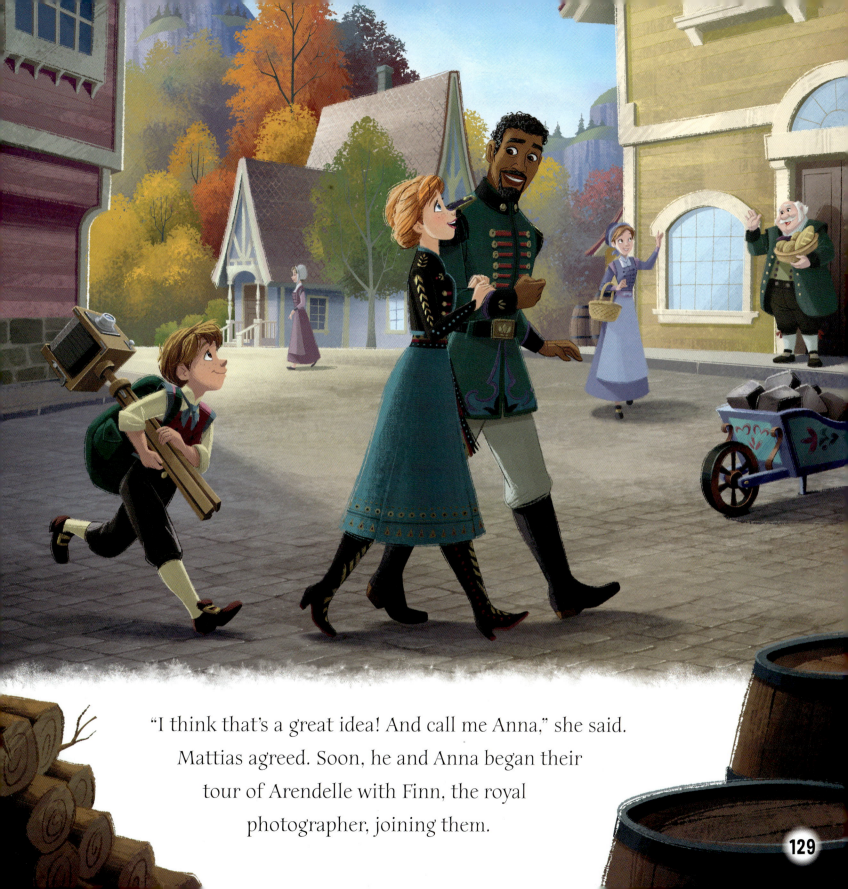

"I think that's a great idea! And call me Anna," she said.
Mattias agreed. Soon, he and Anna began their
tour of Arendelle with Finn, the royal
photographer, joining them.

Anna and Mattias stopped first at the town square.

"I used to sail paper boats in this fountain," said Anna.

"So did your father," said Mattias, smiling. "I saw him here on occasion fishing soggy boats from the water. Whenever I came to the town square with my father, we stopped here, too. He would let me toss in coins and make a wish."

Welcome Home

Just then, a familiar smell caught Mattias's attention.

Anna took a whiff and instantly recognised the overpowering odour of lutefisk coming from the fishmonger's shop.

"That brings back memories," she said.

Mattias's face softened. "My parents served fish almost every day. Dried fish, fish soups, smoked fish."

Anna giggled. "That is a lot of fish!"

Mattias nodded. "What I wouldn't give for a big meal with my family right now."

"Would you settle for a fish-kabab with me instead?" asked Anna.

The two went inside the shop and enjoyed a snack.

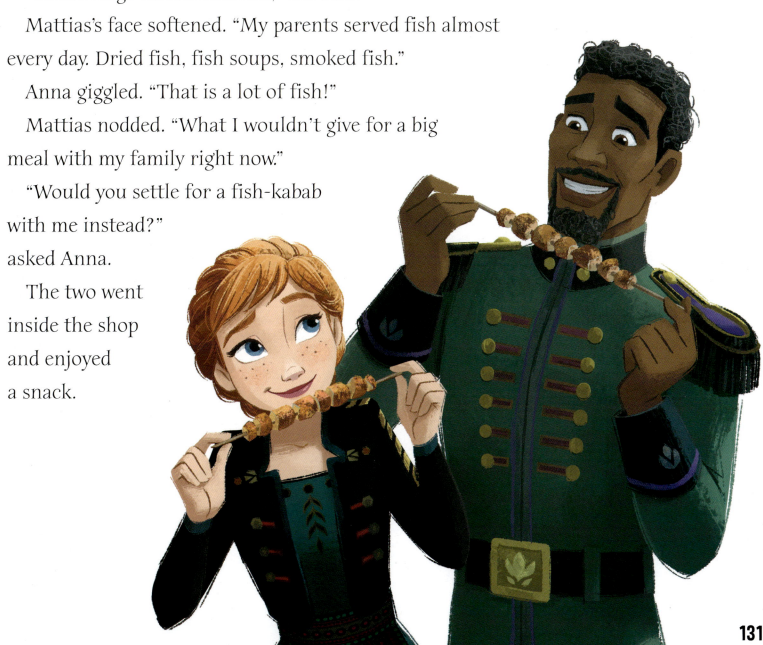

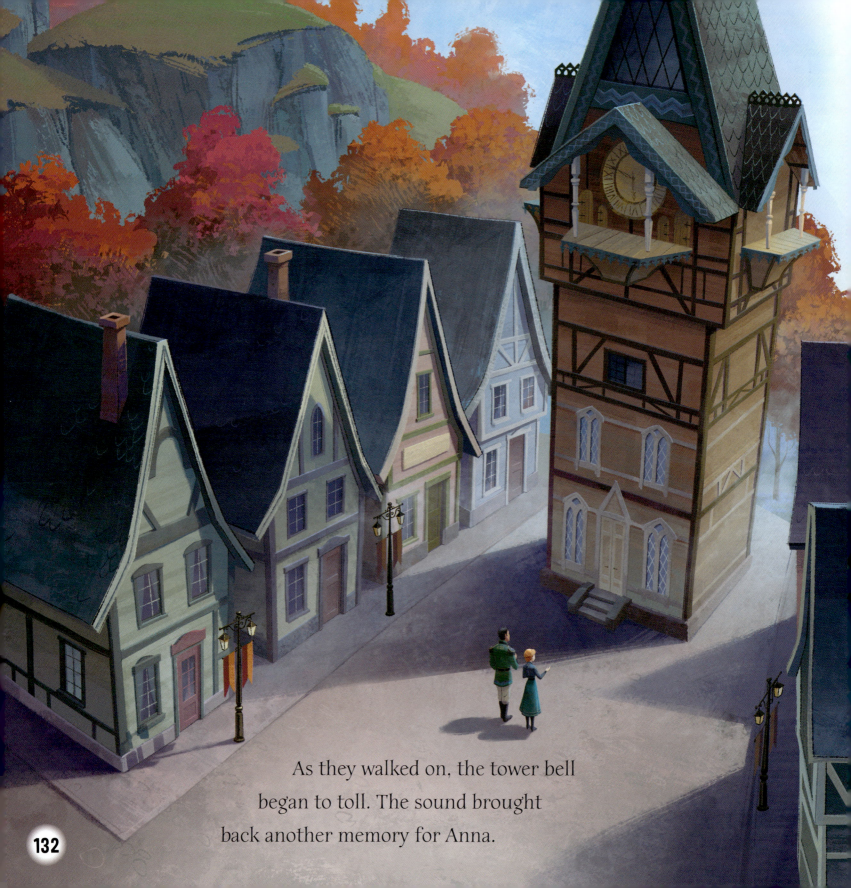

As they walked on, the tower bell
began to toll. The sound brought
back another memory for Anna.

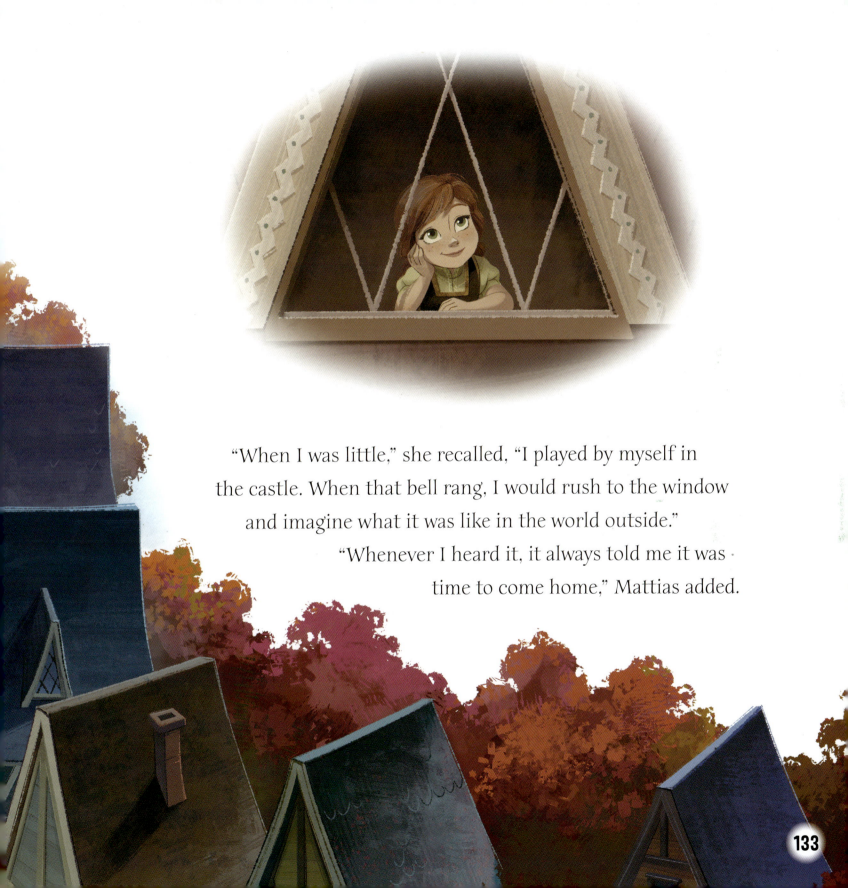

"When I was little," she recalled, "I played by myself in the castle. When that bell rang, I would rush to the window and imagine what it was like in the world outside."

"Whenever I heard it, it always told me it was time to come home," Mattias added.

They walked the rest of the day, rediscovering the Arendelle they had called home since they were children. As the sun began to hide behind the mountains, their path led them past the new statue of King Agnarr and Queen Iduna as young children.

Welcome Home

Mattias and Anna stopped at the same time.

"I miss them," Anna said quietly.

Mattias knew how she felt. "My father always said, never take the good for granted, because just when you think you've found your way, life will throw you onto a new path."

Anna smiled in wonder as she reflected on the amazing journey from the castle… to the Enchanted Forest… and finally to the throne as Arendelle's new queen.

Welcome Home

"We've both been on quite a path, Mattias," Anna said.

"Indeed, Your Maj– Anna," he replied. "It's been quite an adventure."

"And in the end, it led us to the most wonderful place of all: home," said Anna.

Later, Anna and Mattias looked at the photos they had taken that day. A lot certainly had changed. But fortunately, the most important things, like friendship, the love of family and the feeling of home, never would.

138